REMY AND RUBY'S RESCUE RANCH

Can't We Be Friends?

By Katy Duffield

Illustrated by
Hazel Quintanilla

Rourke
Educational Media
rourkeeducationalmedia.com

A Division of
Carson
Dellosa
Education

Dear Guardian/Educator,
Introduce your child to the wonderful world of reading with our leveled readers. Your growing reader will be continuously engaged as he or she is guided from one level to the next. Each level is carefully built to provide your child with the reading skills and knowledge to be a confident reader! Ultimately, we want your child to develop a love of reading.

Level 1 *Learning to Read*
High frequency words, basic sentences, large type, labels, full color illustrations to help young readers better comprehend the text

Level 2 *Beginning to Read Alone*
Short sentences, familiar words, simple plot, easy-to-read fonts

Level 3 *Reading on Your Own*
Short paragraphs, easy-to-follow plots, vocabulary is increasingly challenging, exciting stories

Level 4 *Proficient Reader*
Chapters, engaging stories, challenging vocabulary, multiple text features

Reading should be a pleasurable experience. A child who enjoys reading reads more, and a child who reads more becomes a better reader. Your child will grow with exposure to broad vocabulary and literary techniques, and will develop deeper critical thinking and comprehension skills. We are excited to be a part of your child's reading journey.

Happy reading,
Rourke Educational Media

© 2020 Rourke Educational Media

All rights reserved. No part of this book may be reproduced or utilized in any form or by any means, electronic or mechanical including photocopying, recording, or by any information storage and retrieval system without permission in writing from the publisher.

www.rourkeeducationalmedia.com

Edited by: Kim Thompson
Cover layout by: Rhea Magaro-Wallace
Interior layout by: Kathy Walsh
Cover and interior illustrations by: Hazel Quintanilla

Library of Congress PCN Data

Can't We Be Friends? / Katy Duffield
(Remy and Ruby's Rescue Ranch)
ISBN 978-1-73161-495-7 (hard cover)(alk. paper)
ISBN 978-1-73161-302-8 (soft cover)
ISBN 978-1-73161-600-5 (e-Book)
ISBN 978-1-73161-705-7 (ePub)
Library of Congress Control Number: 2019932392

Printed in the United States of America,
North Mankato, Minnesota

Table of Contents

Chapter One
Meet Yoshi

"Look who's here!" Auntie
Red calls.

Remy and Ruby run toward
the outdoor pen.

"Cool!" Remy cries.

"That is the biggest turtle I

have ever seen," Ruby says.

"She is a **tortoise**," Auntie Red says. "Her name is Yoshi."

Ruby and Remy move closer. They run their fingers over her bumpy shell.

"She is HUGE!" Remy says.

"Can we let her swim in the **pond**?" Ruby asks.

"Nope," Auntie Red says. "Tortoises live on land."

She points at Yoshi's front feet. "See? She doesn't have any flippers to help her swim."

PuSh. PuSh. PuSh.

Yoshi pushes her way across
the ground. She **chomps** big
bites of grass.

"She's fast!" Remy says.

WOOF! WOOF! WOOF!

The ranch dog, Little Joe,

barks and barks.

"Little Joe!" Ruby cries.

"What's wrong with you?"

Little Joe growls. He shows

his teeth.

"I don't think Little Joe likes

Yoshi," Remy says.

Chapter Two

Barks and Hisses

Ruby holds out her hand.

"Come here, boy," she calls.

But Little Joe doesn't come.

He runs up and down the
fence. He barks and howls.

After a while, Joe comes

closer.

JUMP! He hops at Yoshi.

Yoshi **hisses**. Then she

tucks her head in her shell.

"Little Joe!" Remy cries.

"You're scaring her!"

Ruby holds Little Joe. She
pats his head.

Remy rubs Yoshi's shell.

"How can we get them to be friends?" Ruby asks.

"It will just take some time," Auntie Red says.

On Sunday, Little Joe barks
at Yoshi. But not as much.

On Monday, Little Joe sniffs
Yoshi's shell.

Yoshi hides her head.

On Tuesday, Little Joe **trots** around Yoshi.

Little by little, Yoshi peeks out...

But then, **WOOF! WOOF!**

Yoshi hides her head again.

"This is not working," Ruby
says.

Chapter Three
Something in Common

"I wish Yoshi and Little Joe

liked each other," Ruby says.

"Me, too," Remy says.

"We should show them how
to be friends," Ruby says.

Remy gets the soccer ball.

He and Ruby play together.

Kick! Kick! Kick!

Soon, Little Joe joins in. He
runs after the ball.

Chase! Chase! Chase!

Then Yoshi joins in too. She

pushes the ball with her head.

PuSh! PuSh! PuSh!

Kick! Kick! Kick!
Chase! Chase! Chase!
Push! Push! Push!

Yoshi goes this way. Little
Joe goes that way. Then Yoshi
and Little Joe stop. They
stand nose to nose.

"Uh-oh," Ruby says.

"Oh, no," Remy says.

But it's all good...

SLURP!

After that, Remy and Ruby...

Kick! Kick! Kick!

Yoshi and Little Joe...

Chase! Chase! Chase!

Push! Push! Push!

The friends play and play
and play—until they can't
play anymore.

Bonus Stuff!

Glossary

chomps (chawmpz): Chews or bites on something.

hisses (HIS-sez): Makes a long *sss* sound to show dislike.

pond (pahnd): An enclosed body of water that is smaller than a lake.

tortoise (TOR-tuhs): A kind of turtle that lives on land.

trots (trahtz): Moves in a way that is faster than a walk, but slower than a run.

Discussion Questions

1. Why do you think Little Joe barked at Yoshi?
2. What do Remy and Ruby do to show Little Joe and Yoshi how to be friends?
3. What did you think would happen when Little Joe and Yoshi came face to face? Were you right or wrong?

Animal Facts: Tortoises

1. Some tortoises can live to be more than 100 years old.

2. Their strong shells can protect them from predators.

3. Tortoises love to eat.

4. Tortoises eat mostly leaves and grasses, but they like flowers too.

5. Tortoises don't swim, but they like to sit in puddles.

6. Baby tortoises hatch from eggs that mother tortoises bury underground.

7. Tortoises like to dig.

8. A tortoise's shell is called a *carapace*.

Creativity Corner

Yoshi and Little Joe have something in common: They both like playing ball. Write a story about something two friends have in common. What adventure does their shared interest lead them on?

About the Author

Katy Duffield is a writer who lives in Arkansas. She's never seen a tortoise as big as Yoshi. But she did have a dog named Little Joe!

About the Illustrator

Hazel Quintanilla loves her job, pajamas, burgers, sketch books, fluffy socks, and of course animals! Hazel had a ton of fun illustrating *Remy and Ruby's Rescue Ranch*.